FRESNO PACIFIC COLLEGE
1717 SOUTH CHESTNUT AVENUE
FRESNO, CALIFORNIA 93702

TEACHER EDUCATION

SCIENCE
QUESTIONS & ANSWERS

Body Science

Anita Ganeri

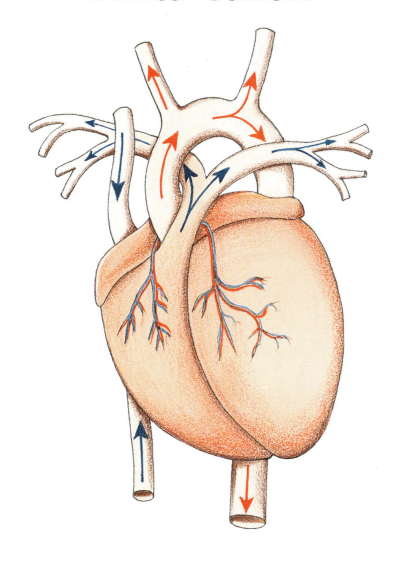

Dillon Press

New York

For my father

First American publication 1993 by Dillon Press, Macmillan Publishing Company,
866 Third Avenue, New York, NY 10022

Macmillan Publishing Company is part of the Maxwell Communication Group of Companies.

First published by Evans Brothers Limited,
2A Portman Mansions, Chiltern Street, London W1M 1LE

Printed in Hong Kong by Wing King Tong Co., Ltd.

10   9   8   7   6   5   4   3   2   1

Library of Congress Cataloging-in-Publication Data

Ganeri, Anita, 1961-
   Body science / Anita Ganeri.
      p.   cm. — (Science questions & answers)
   Includes bibliographical references and index.
   Summary: Illustrations and explanatory text answer questions about the human
body and how it works.
   ISBN 0-87518-576-2
   1. Human physiology—Juvenile literature.   2. Human anatomy—Juvenile literature.
3. Body, Human—Juvenile literature.
   [1. Body,   Human—Miscellanea.   2. Questions and answers.]   I. Title.   II. Series.
   QP37.G33   1993
   612—dc20   92-22722

Acknowledgments

The author and publishers would like to thank the following
people for their valuable help and advice:

Dr. Purim Ganeri, MBBS, MRCP, MRCCP, DCH
Sally Morgan, MA, MSc, MIBiol

Illustrations: Virginia Gray
Editors: Catherine Chambers and Jean Coppendale
Design: Monica Chia
Production: Jenny Mulvanny

For permission to reproduce copyright material, the author and publishers gratefully acknowledge the following:
Cover photographs:(top left) A sweat pore, Dr Jeremy Burgess / Science Photo Library, (bottom left) Surface of the skin showing
a hair, CNRI / Science Photo Library, (top right) An adult brain, Petit Format, J D Dauple / Science Photo Library, (bottom right)
Close-up of an eye, Martin Dohrn / Science Photo Library.
page 6 - (top) Dr Manfred Kage, Bruce Coleman Limited, (bottom) Alfred Pasieka, Bruce Coleman Limited; page 8 - Dr Manfred Kage
/ Science Photo Library; page 10 - John Garrett, Bubbles; page 11 - (left) Hutchison Library, (right) David Campione / Science Photo
Library; page 13 - (top) G & M David De Lossy, The Image Bank, (bottom) Hank Morgan / Science Photo Library, (inset) Lois Joy
Thurston, Bubbles; page 14 - Jerry Mason / Science Photo Library; page 15 - (top) Eric Grave / Science Photo Library, (bottom) Sally
Morgan, Ecoscene; page 20 - Robert Harding Picture Library; page 21 - Sally Morgan, Ecoscene; page 22 - (left) Terje Rakke, The Image
Bank, (right) Gerold Jung, The Image Bank; page 24 - Jacques Cochin, The Image Bank; page 27 - (top left) Philip Kretchmar, The
Image Bank, (bottom left) Steve Niedorf, The Image Bank, (top right) Sally Morgan, Ecoscene, (middle) Adrien Duey, The Image Bank,
(bottom right) Nino Mascardi, The Image Bank; page 28 - Petit Format, J D Dauple / Science Photo Library; page 29 - Sally Morgan,
Ecoscene; page 30 - Sally Morgan, Ecoscene; page 31 - (top) J G Fuller, Hutchison Library, (middle & bottom) Biophoto Associates;
page 33 - (left) Biophoto Associates, (right) Danny Brass / Science Photo Library; page 34 - Adam Hart-Davis / Science Photo Library;
page 37 - Leo Mason, The Image Bank; page 39 - (top left) Sally Morgan, Ecoscene, (bottom left) Ian West, Bubbles, (top right) Hans
Reinhard, Bruce Coleman Limited; page 40 - M I Walker / Science Photo Library; page 42 - (top) Norman Tomalin, Bruce Coleman
Limited, (bottom) Maria Productions, The Image Bank; page 43 - (left) The Image Bank, (right) Biophoto Associates; page 44 - Ira
Block, The Image Bank; page 45 - (left) Nicholas Devore, Bruce Coleman Limited, (right) Lucy Durrell McKenna, Biophoto Associates.

Contents

What are you made of?

Take a good, long look at yourself. How many parts of your body can you name? Bones, muscles, skin, nails, heart – these are just a few to start with. There are many more, all working together to make your body function properly.

So what are you made of? Your body is about two-thirds water. In an adult man, this is about ten gallons of water, enough to fill 120 soda cans. But your bones, muscles, skin, and so on are made of tiny living things called cells. You are made of about 50 billion of these little building blocks.

Cells come in different shapes and sizes, and each type has a different job to do. For example, red blood cells are tiny and shaped like doughnuts. Nerve cells have long, thin, trailing "tails."

Groups of the same types of cell make up **body tissue**. There are different kinds, such as muscle tissue and skin tissue. Groups of different types of tissue form organs, such as your heart or lungs. Each organ has its own special job to do in your body.

Most of your cells are repaired or replaced as they die or wear out. Bone cells last for years, but the cells lining part of your digestive tube, in your stomach, only live for two to three days. Red blood cells, however, live for about four months. The only cells that are not replaced when they die are those that make your nerves . . . and your brain.

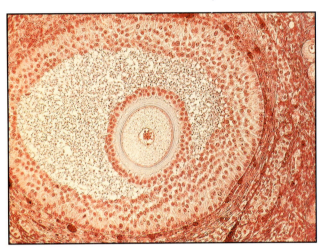

Female egg cells, or ova, are stored inside a woman's ovaries. They are about 0.004 – 0.008 inch wide.

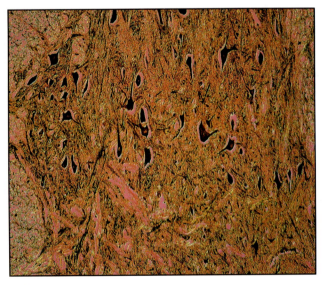

This photo shows nerve cells from the spinal cord. They help you move. They are shown magnified by 64 times.

 Did you know?

Most cells are too small to be seen except under a microscope. The biggest cells are female egg cells. They can just be seen with the naked eye. Some of the smallest cells are in your brain. They are just $\frac{1}{500}$ inch across. Hundreds would fit on the period that ends this sentence.

What is a cell made of?

cell membrane
the cell's outer layer; it keeps the cell's shape and lets oxygen and **nutrients** in and **waste products** out.

cytoplasm
the jellylike main part of the cell; it is about two-thirds water, with some **protein**.

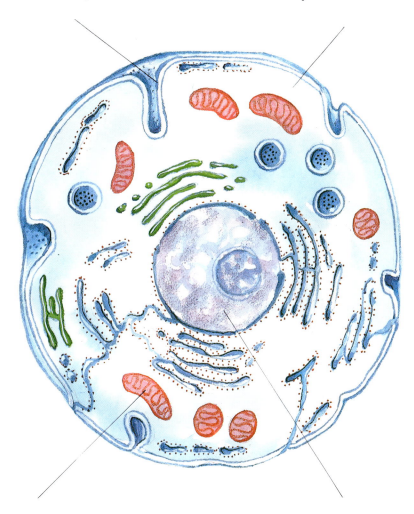

There are lots of other small particles that cannot be seen underneath an ordinary microscope. They have many different jobs to do. This particle is a mitochondrion (mitochondria). Mitochondria are the cell's power supplies. They make the energy to keep the cell working.

nucleus
the center of the cell's body and its controller. It contains special threads, called chromosomes. They carry coded instructions, called genes, that tell the cell how to work.

7

What are bones for?

There are lots of bones inside your body. They make up your skeleton. Bones are tough and strong. But they can also bend slightly so that they do not break too easily. Your skeleton holds your body up and keeps its shape. Without it, you would collapse on the floor.

Some bones help protect the soft, delicate parts of your body. The spine, or backbone, protects your main nerves. The skull protects your brain, and the ribs protect your heart and your lungs.

Bones also help you move. They cannot bend very much, so your body has joints where it can twist and turn. There are joints at your knees, ankles, elbows, and shoulders. Your knee and elbow joints act a bit like hinges on a door so that you can bend your legs and arms.

In a joint, two bones meet and are held in place by strong, stretchy straps called ligaments. The ends of each bone are covered in tough, shiny cartilage, a kind of cushion that stops bones from rubbing or wearing out. The joint is kept well oiled by a liquid called synovial fluid.

Your skeleton provides a tough framework for your body. The bones hold you up, rather like scaffolding around a building. They also protect the soft organs inside your body from injury. The joints between your bones and the muscles attached to them allow you to move freely.

 Did you know?

Your biggest bones are in your thighs. Your smallest bones are in your ears. An adult has about 206 bones in the body, but a baby has more than 300. Some of these bones join together as the baby gets older.

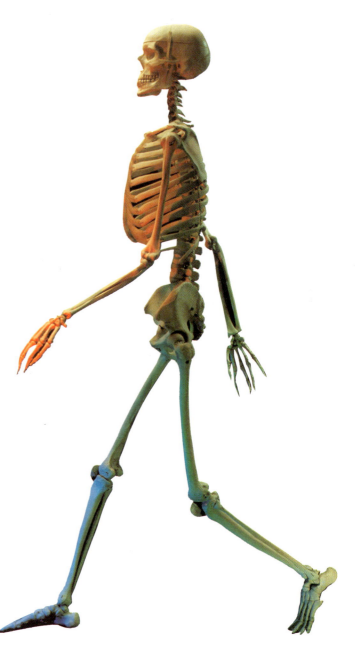

8

Here you can see some of the main bones in your skeleton. They all have scientific names. But many also have common names that you may already know.

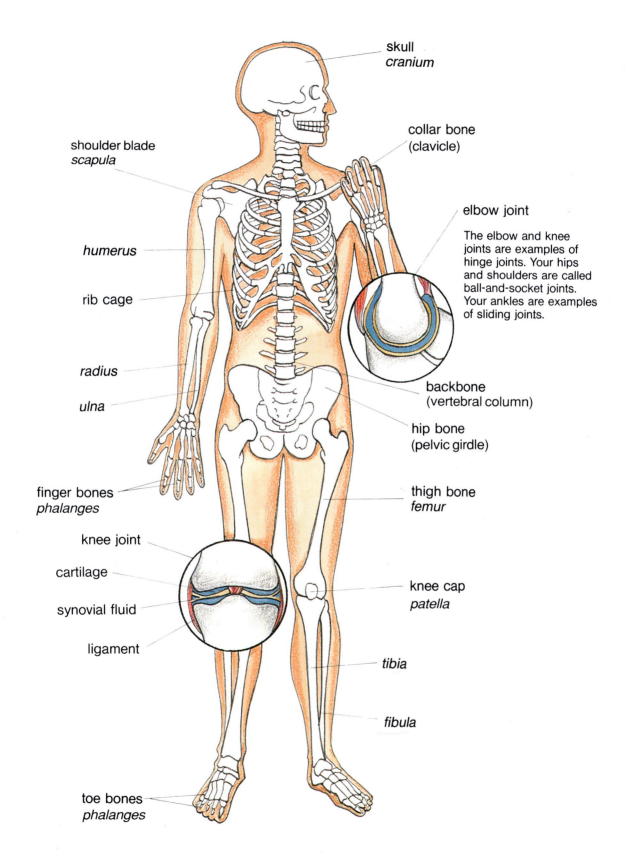

skull
cranium

collar bone
(clavicle)

elbow joint

The elbow and knee joints are examples of hinge joints. Your hips and shoulders are called ball-and-socket joints. Your ankles are examples of sliding joints.

shoulder blade
scapula

humerus

rib cage

radius

ulna

backbone
(vertebral column)

hip bone
(pelvic girdle)

finger bones
phalanges

thigh bone
femur

knee joint

cartilage

synovial fluid

ligament

knee cap
patella

tibia

fibula

toe bones
phalanges

What are muscles for?

Muscles work with bones so that you can move. Muscles are **supple** and strong. They have long strips at each end that fix them to bones. These are called tendons. There is a big tendon at the back of your heel. Can you feel it? It is called your Achilles tendon.

When you want to move, your brain sends a message to your muscles. It tells them to get shorter, or contract. As they contract, they pull on the bone and move it. This is how your elbow bends or your head nods.

You have hundreds of muscles under your skin. They often work in pairs to move different parts of your body. To move your elbow one way, one muscle gets shorter and the other relaxes. To move it the other way, the muscles change jobs.

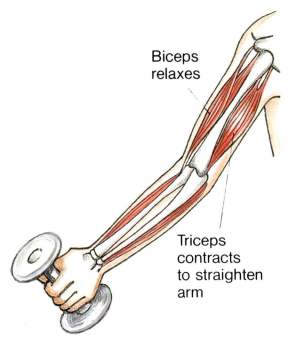

Biceps relaxes

Triceps contracts to straighten arm

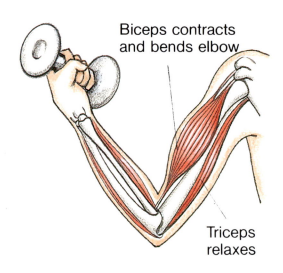

Biceps contracts and bends elbow

Triceps relaxes

These upper-arm muscles work in pairs to move the lower arm up or down. When one muscle contracts, the other relaxes.

You use hundreds of different muscles when you play soccer.

 Did you know?

You have about 650 muscles in your body. The biggest are in your buttocks and the smallest are in your ear. You use an amazing 200 muscles when you walk.

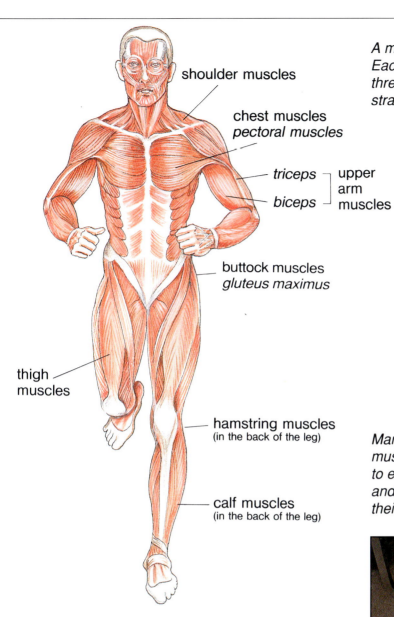

shoulder muscles

chest muscles
pectoral muscles

triceps ⌉ upper
        arm
biceps ⌋ muscles

buttock muscles
gluteus maximus

thigh
muscles

hamstring muscles
(in the back of the leg)

calf muscles
(in the back of the leg)

A muscle is made up of bundles of muscle fibers. Each fiber, in turn, is made up of even tinier threads called myofibrils. They are made up of strands of protein.

Inside a muscle

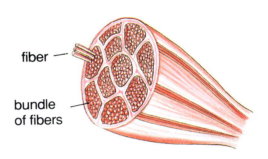

fiber

bundle
of fibers

Many people work very hard to keep their muscles in good shape. Some people lift weights to exercise their muscles and make them bigger and stronger. Athletes have to train hard to keep their muscles strong.

Most muscles are only known by their scientific names. Some also have common names. Muscles lie in layers all over your body just under your skin.

11

Why does your heart beat?

Your body needs nutrients from food, and oxygen from the air to make it work properly. These are carried to all parts of the body by your blood. The blood also takes away waste products, such as carbon dioxide gas, which could poison your cells. Blood has to be pushed around your body all the time, and this is where your heart comes in. It acts like a muscle pump, sending blood around your body with every beat.

Your heart beats about 80 to 90 times a minute. With each beat, the left side of your heart pumps blood from your lungs, where it collects a supply of oxygen, to the rest of your body. The right side pumps stale blood from your body to your lungs for more oxygen. Special flaplike valves in your heart snap shut after the blood has gone through. This stops it from flowing backward. The valves make a rhythmic sound as they close. This is your heartbeat.

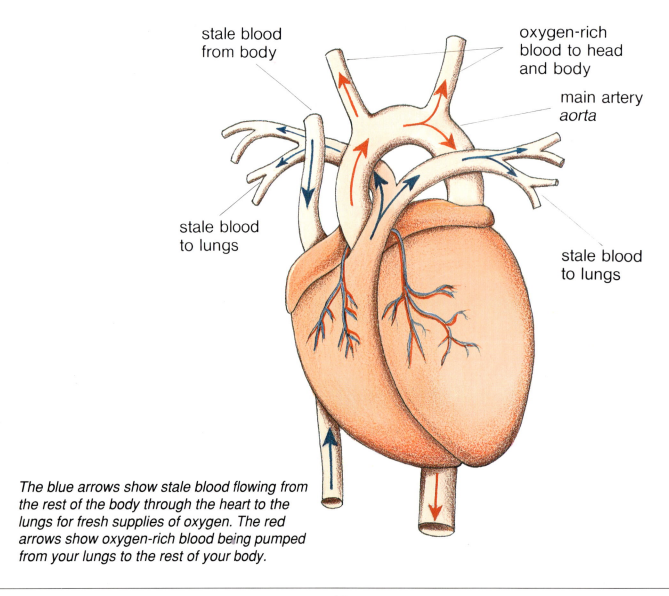

stale blood
from body

oxygen-rich
blood to head
and body

main artery
aorta

stale blood
to lungs

stale blood
to lungs

The blue arrows show stale blood flowing from the rest of the body through the heart to the lungs for fresh supplies of oxygen. The red arrows show oxygen-rich blood being pumped from your lungs to the rest of your body.

Jogging or cycling helps make your heart and lungs stronger and improves your blood circulation. They are called aerobic forms of exercise. They increase your ability to get oxygen around your body.

 ## Did you know?

Your clenched fist is about the size of an adult's heart. The heart is made of a special type of muscle, called cardiac muscle. Unlike the type of muscle in your arms and legs, it never stops working while you are alive.

 ## Did you know?

When you are resting, about one cupful of blood is pumped around your body with every three beats of your heart. When you exercise, about two cupfuls are pumped with just one beat.

 ## See for yourself

Each time your heart beats, blood surges or rushes through your body. You can feel this surge when you take your pulse. This measures how often your heart beats each minute. Press the inside of one wrist with the middle fingers of your other hand. Can you feel a gentle throbbing? This is your blood surging through your wrist. Use a watch to count the number of surges in one minute. The number of surges you count is called your pulse rate. Do this twice: first after you have been sitting quietly for a while and then after you have been running around. You should have very different pulse rates.

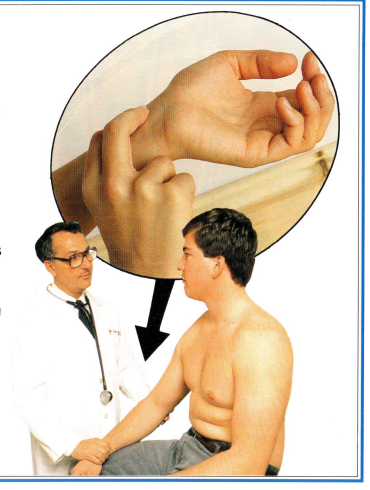

What is blood made of?

Like everything else in your body, blood is made of cells. These float around in a sticky, cloudy yellow liquid called plasma. It is about nine-tenths water, with added chemicals and nutrients.

Plasma makes up over half of your blood. The rest consists of red and white blood cells, and platelets. Red blood cells are tiny, among the smallest cells in your body. But there are a great many of them – about 12.5 billion in all. Their job is to carry oxygen around your body.

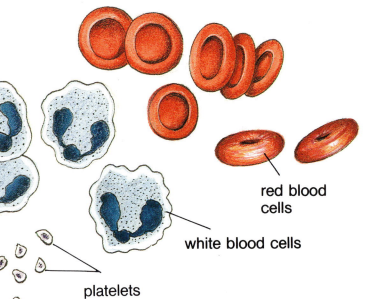

red blood cells

white blood cells

platelets

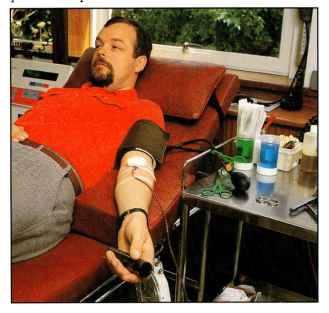

There are several types of white cells in your blood. They are all bigger than the red cells. Their main job is to destroy harmful germs. Last, but not least, come the platelets. These are tiny fragments, or pieces, of cell. If you cut yourself, they help your blood to clot so that it seals the wound. You have about ten pints of blood in your body – about half a bucketful.

Blood flows around your body through a system of tubes called arteries, veins, and capillaries. You have about 60,000 miles of these **blood vessels** inside you.

 Did you know?

Red blood cells and many white cells are made in the jellylike substance called marrow that is inside many of your bones. When old cells die, the marrow replaces them. It produces an amazing 2 million new red blood cells every second.

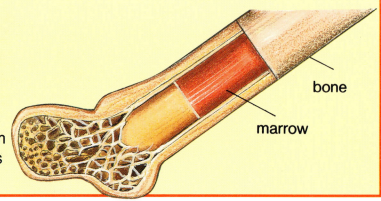

bone

marrow

Why is blood red?

Your red blood cells contain a special substance called hemoglobin, which carries oxygen around your body and also gives blood its red color. As your blood flows through your lungs, the hemoglobin takes in oxygen and carries it throughout your body. When the hemoglobin is filled with fresh oxygen, it looks red.

As blood travels through you and the hemoglobin uses up its oxygen supply, it turns purply blue. The veins on the back of your hand look blue because they are carrying this stale blood back to your heart and lungs.

 Did you know?

If you prick yourself with a pin, the drop of blood that appears contains about 2.5 million red blood cells, 5,000 white blood cells, and 250,000 platelets.

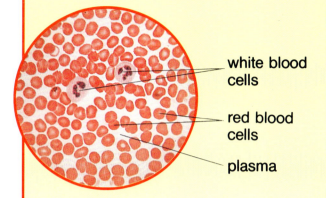

white blood cells

red blood cells

plasma

 See for yourself

Try making a model blood sample to see how the blood cells float around in the plasma. Fill a screw-top jar with some warm water. Do not use hot water. Stir in a teaspoonful of sugar to make the plasma. Then add 3 teaspoonfuls of tea leaves for the blood cells. Put the top on the jar and shake it.

The tea leaves will flow around in the sugar water, like blood cells in plasma. If you stop shaking the jar, most of the tea leaves will sink to the bottom. Your blood cells do not sink because your blood is constantly moving.

The jar of "plasma" has been shaken. You can see that some of the tea leaves have settled.

What do your kidneys do?

Your two kidneys **filter** your blood to get rid of any waste substances. The product is a liquid called **urine**. This travels down two tubes, called ureters, into your bladder. The bladder is like a muscular bag. When you go to the bathroom, urine is passed out of your body through the urethra.

Your body cannot work properly without fluids. Kidneys help control the amount of fluids that you have, so if you have not had a drink for a long time, your kidneys do not make much urine. But if you drink too much, the kidneys make a lot of urine and you urinate more frequently.

Your kidneys are in the lower part of your body, just below your last pair of ribs. Blood from your body flows into your kidneys through the renal artery. When it has been cleaned, it flows back into the rest of your body through the renal vein. The word renal *is the scientific word for anything to do with kidneys.*

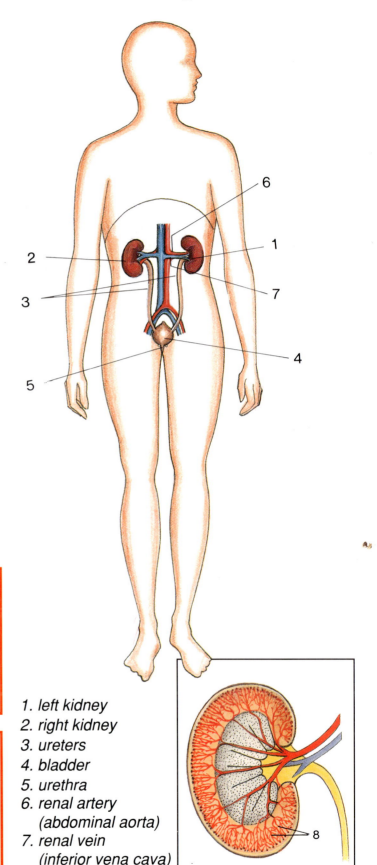

1. left kidney
2. right kidney
3. ureters
4. bladder
5. urethra
6. renal artery
   (abdominal aorta)
7. renal vein
   (inferior vena cava)
8. blood vessels

 Did you know?

An average person makes about 11,000 gallons of urine in his or her lifetime. Your bladder can hold 1 pint of urine before you need to go to the bathroom.

 Did you know?

Your kidneys are about 4 inches long and 1$\frac{1}{2}$ inches wide. They contain about one million tiny filters, called nephrons.

What does your liver do?

Your liver does several very important jobs. It makes a green liquid called bile, which is stored in the gallbladder. Bile helps break down fats in the food that you digest so that your body can use them. When your food has been digested, your blood becomes full of nutrients. The blood takes a detour through the liver before passing through the rest of your body. The liver stores some of the nutrients and changes others into forms that are more useful to your body.

Your liver also gets rid of some of the poisonous substances in food or drink. It turns the poisons into harmless substances. This process is called detoxification.

The liver controls the amount of **glucose** in your blood. It also destroys worn-out blood cells and makes important blood proteins.

Your pancreas makes a chemical called insulin. It works with the liver to control the level of sugar in your bloodstream. Your pancreas also makes juices that help you digest your food.

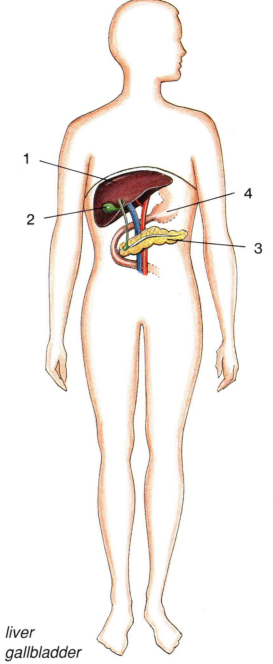

1. *liver*
2. *gallbladder*
3. *pancreas*
4. *stomach*

 Did you know?

Your liver has amazing powers of recovery. Up to 90 percent of it can be destroyed before it is irreversibly damaged. The other 10 percent of the liver can grow back to a normal size.

 Did you know?

The liver is your biggest organ. In an adult it weighs over three pounds.

How do you breathe?

Just as a car needs gasoline, your body needs oxygen, a gas from the air, to make it work properly. Without oxygen, your cells would die in a few minutes. Cells also make a waste gas called carbon dioxide. The cells need to get rid of this waste gas so that it does not poison them. This is why you breathe – to supply your cells with oxygen and take away waste.

You breathe all the time, automatically. Air goes in through your nose or mouth, down your windpipe (trachea), then down two tubes (bronchi) into your lungs. In each lung, these tubes branch again and again, rather like a tree. At the end of each branch is a tiny bubblelike structure called an air sac, or **alveolus**.

The air sacs (alveoli) are covered with fine blood vessels. Oxygen passes from the alveoli into your blood and is then carried around your body. Waste carbon dioxide passes the other way, to be breathed out.

When you breathe in, your ribs move up and out to give your lungs room to expand as you suck in air. Your diaphragm (the sheet of muscle across your chest, under your lungs) also moves down to make more space. When you breathe out, your ribs move in and down, and your diaphragm moves upward. This makes the space in your chest smaller and helps squeeze air out.

Breathing in

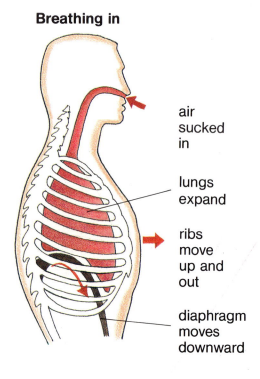

air sucked in

lungs expand

ribs move up and out

diaphragm moves downward

Breathing out

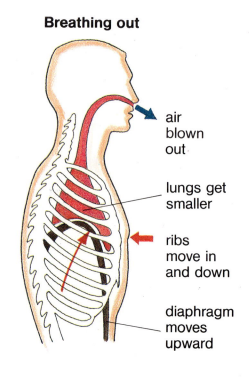

air blown out

lungs get smaller

ribs move in and down

diaphragm moves upward

Why do you pant when you have been running?

When you exercise, your muscles work harder and need more oxygen than usual. Your brain tells you to breathe quicker to get enough oxygen to your muscles. Panting helps you take in more air.

The lungs

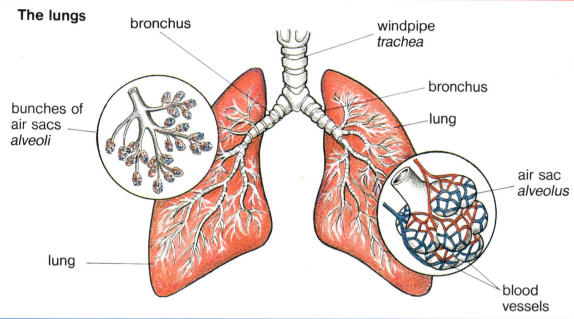

bronchus

windpipe *trachea*

bunches of air sacs *alveoli*

bronchus

lung

air sac *alveolus*

lung

blood vessels

See for yourself

To see how big your breaths are, you will need a big plastic milk container and a length of plastic tubing. Fill the container up by dipping it into a sink full of water. Then tip it upside down quickly, in the sink, without lifting it out of the water. Make sure that the container stays full. Put one end of the tube under it and breathe out through the other end. Your breaths will force some of the water out of the container. Do this ten times, then mark the level of water on the container with a ballpoint pen.

Now you can see how the air in each breath replaced a certain volume, or amount of water in the container. Empty the container and fill it up to the mark you made, with more water from the tap.

The water represents the air that you breathed out. Now you can pour that water into a measuring cup to see how many ounces of air you breathed out. Divide the number of ounces by ten to give you the volume of each breath. Now you know how big each breath is.

Why do you sneeze?

You sneeze when you have a cold or if you are allergic, or react badly, to dust or flower pollen in the air. Sometimes you seem to sneeze for no reason at all. But sneezing does have a useful purpose. You sneeze to blow irritating dust or mucus (a slimy substance produced when you have a cold) out of your nose and to clear your breathing passages. Have you ever tried to stop yourself from sneezing? It is very difficult to do because sneezing is an **automatic reaction**. When you sneeze, your throat closes and air builds up in your lungs. Suddenly, the air explodes out of your nose.

What makes you cough?

Coughing also helps to clear blockages in your throat, lungs, and breathing tubes. When you cough, your vocal cords close and the muscles in your chest squeeze, building up the pressure of air in your lungs. When the pressure is too great, your vocal cords open and the air rushes out of your mouth. It carries with it any irritating bits of dust or mucus, and hopefully allows you to breathe more easily again.

 Did you know?

Coughs and sneezes travel at high speed. You normally breathe air out at about 5 miles per hour. In a cough, the air travels at about 60 miles per hour. In a sneeze, the air is forced out at up to 100 miles per hour.

 Did you know?

The longest sneezing fit lasted more than 2 ½ years. The person sneezed about one million times in the first year, that is, about 2,740 times a day.

 See for yourself

Coughs and sneezes can spread diseases when you have a cold. A sneeze contains about 100,000 tiny droplets of mucus, full of cold germs. When the germs are exploded into the air, other people can easily breathe them in if you do not catch them in a handkerchief. To see how a sneeze spreads germs, you will need a large sheet of paper, a drinking straw, and a cup of water that has been colored with food dye. Make sure that you, and everything around you, are well covered.

Suck up some water through the straw. Stand about 3 feet away from the paper and blow the water hard at the paper. The splatters of color are like the mucus drops in a sneeze. How far have they spread over the paper?

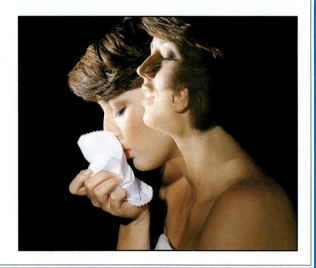

What causes hiccups?

Your diaphragm is the flat sheet of muscle under your ribs, which you use for breathing. You get hiccups when it contracts, or squeezes, more violently than normal. This causes you to breathe in with short gasps of air. Your vocal cords close suddenly and make the "hic" sound you hear.

No one knows exactly why hiccups start. But even unborn babies get them. You may get hiccups if you have eaten or drunk too quickly or too much.

The hiccups usually stop quite quickly, but people have thought up plenty of weird and wonderful cures. They include holding your breath, scaring the person who has the hiccups, or trying to drink a glass of water from the wrong side of the glass. This may not cure your hiccups, but you might forget about them for a while as you dry off.

This is one of the ways that people try to cure their hiccups. Do you think it will work or will you just get a wet face?

Why do you get a "stitch"?

Do you ever get a sharp, stabbing pain in your side when you are running or doing exercise? This is known as a "stitch." It is caused when your diaphragm gets a cramp, or tightens up. This happens when you suddenly begin doing strenuous exercise, and so you start breathing more quickly. Your diaphragm suddenly has to work much harder than normal, and you may get a stitch.

The pain usually goes away after a few minutes. If it does not go, bend down and touch your toes to stretch and relax your diaphragm. You may get

 Did you know?

The longest attack of hiccuping on record began in 1922 . . . and lasted for 70 years! The sufferer led a normal life, but could not wear false teeth, as they would have jumped up and down in his mouth. He hiccuped about 25 times a minute, 1,500 times an hour, 36,000 times a day.

a stitch if you exercise too soon after eating a meal. Always wait at least two hours after eating before you do any strenuous exercise.

How do you speak and sing?

Press the front of your neck gently with your fingers. Can you feel a lump in your throat? This is your voice box (larynx). It is at the top of your windpipe (trachea). Adult men have bigger voice boxes than women or children. They are called "Adam's apples." You can see them quite clearly.

Two bands of cartilage are stretched across your voice box. These are your vocal cords. When you breathe normally, your vocal cords are relaxed and still. There is a large space for air to pass through. But when you speak or sing, your vocal cords tense and tighten. Air rushes past them and makes them **vibrate** very quickly. The vibrations make the basic sounds of speaking and singing. The closer your

The lump on the neck is an Adam's apple, or voice box.

vocal cords are together, the higher the sounds you make. The farther apart they are, the lower the sounds.

To shape the sounds into words, you use your throat muscles, lips, tongue, and teeth. Try saying some of the letters of the alphabet. Which bit of your mouth do you use most?

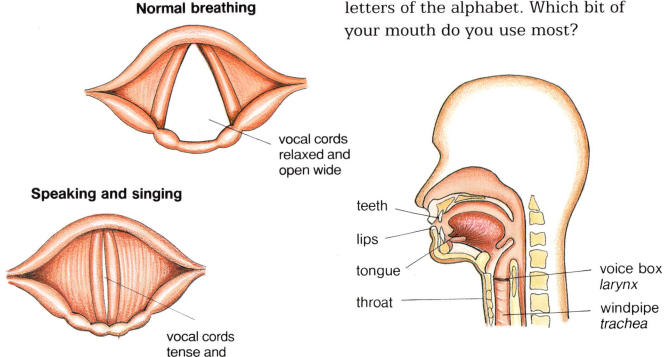

Normal breathing

vocal cords relaxed and open wide

Speaking and singing

vocal cords tense and close together

teeth

lips

tongue

throat

voice box *larynx*

windpipe *trachea*

Why do boys' voices break?

The length and thickness of your vocal cords and the size of your voice box affect how high or deep your voice is. The longer and thicker your vocal cords and the bigger your voice box, the deeper is your voice. When a boy becomes a teenager, his vocal cords grow very quickly. His voice suddenly changes from high to low. This is when his voice is said to "break."

 Did you know?

At birth, your vocal cords are about $1/4$ inch long. They grow to about $3/4$ inch in adult women and to about $1\frac{1}{4}$ inch in adult men.

 Did you know?

About 5,000 different languages are spoken throughout the world. Some 750 million people speak Mandarin Chinese, more than any other language.
The next most commonly spoken language is English, with about 350 million speakers.

 See for yourself

When you are using your voice, the harder you breathe out, the louder are the sounds you make. Try this experiment to see how this works. Start talking and see how long you can continue without taking a breath. Use a clock with a second hand to time yourself. Does your voice get softer and softer as you run out of breath?

Now try shouting for as long as you can without taking a breath. How long can you do this for? You have to breathe out harder when you shout, so you probably have to pause for breath sooner.

Professional singers, such as opera and rock singers, have to learn how to breathe and use their voices in a special way. This is so that they do not damage or strain their vocal cords. They are taught to sing from their diaphragm rather than from their throats. This gives their voices a deeper, richer sound.

Why do you feel hungry?

Everything you do uses up energy. Running and swimming use up lots of energy, but breathing and even blinking use energy, too. You get your energy from the food that you eat. You also get nutrients from food. These help you to grow and to mend worn-out or injured parts of your body.

You get hungry because your supplies of energy and nutrients are running low. A special part of your brain, called the appetite center, detects this. It makes you think that you should eat something, so you feel hungry.

Some foods contain lots of energy. Others contain very little. You could run a 1.2-mile race on the amount of energy in a chocolate bar. But you could only run 55 yards on the energy contained in a lettuce leaf.

1.2 miles

55 yards

Sudden spurts of intense activity use up a lot of energy. Athletes have to follow special diets that are high in protein to build up their muscles, and carbohydrates to give them energy. Protein is found in foods such as fish, meat, and beans. Carbohydrates are found in foods such as bread, rice, and potatoes.

Where does your food go?

When you are enjoying munching an apple or a chocolate bar, you do not stop to think where the food is going or what will happen to it. The food starts a long journey through your body, through a long system of tubes called your digestive system. As it travels, it is broken down into tiny particles, small enough to be **absorbed** by your blood and carried around your body to your cells.

From your mouth, your food travels down a long tube called the esophagus. It does not just slide down, but is pushed by muscles in the esophagus. This pushing is called peristalsis. The power of the muscles means that food can still go down even if you are standing on your head.

The food is pushed into your stomach, where it is mixed with juices and broken down into a souplike mash.

It stays in your stomach for about three hours. Then it travels through your small intestine, where more juices are added. Most of the food is **digested** here, passing through the walls of the intestine and into your bloodstream.

Any undigested, or unwanted, food goes into the next part of your digestive system, the large intestine. This waste is turned into feces and passed through the anus, which is the opening to the exterior of your body.

Your digestive system is about 29 ½ feet long from beginning to end. A meal may take about three days to pass through you. It stays in your stomach for only about three hours.

The digestive system

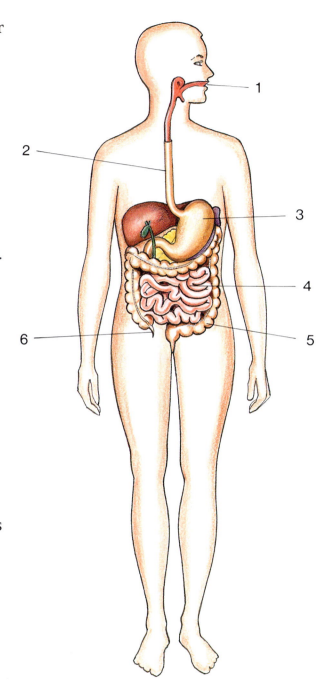

1. *mouth*
2. *esophagus*
3. *stomach*
4. *small intestine*
5. *large intestine*
6. *appendix (see page 27)*

What happens when food goes down "the wrong way"?

When you swallow a piece of food, a flap called the epiglottis covers the top of your windpipe, and the food goes down your esophagus and into your digestive system. But this process can go wrong. If you accidentally breathe in as you swallow the food, the epiglottis opens up. Then the food gets into your windpipe. You may choke on it and have difficulty in breathing properly. This is when food goes down "the wrong way."

Why does your stomach rumble?

Your stomach sometimes rumbles when you are hungry. But not always. It may also rumble as food and air are squeezed through your body, along your digestive tubes.

The wrong way

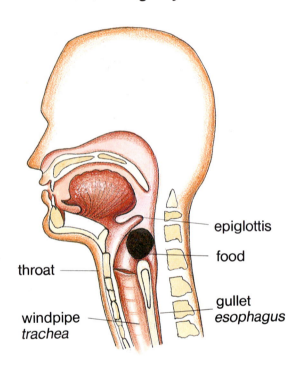

throat

windpipe
trachea

epiglottis

food

gullet
esophagus

The right way

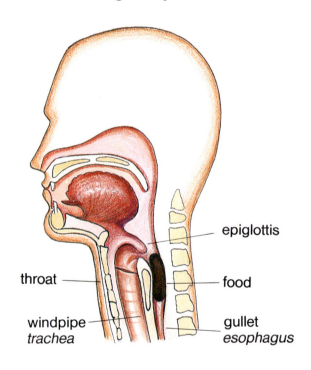

throat

windpipe
trachea

epiglottis

food

gullet
esophagus

 ## See for yourself

The chemicals that break down your food into smaller pieces are called **enzymes**. The saliva, or spit, that you make in your mouth contains enzymes. These break down the **starch** in foods such as potatoes and bread and turn the starch into sugar. The sugar dissolves more easily as it goes down into your stomach. You can see how this enzyme works by keeping a piece of dry bread in your mouth for a few minutes. It will soon taste sweet. You make more than a quart of saliva every day.

Which foods are good for you?

You need to eat a balanced diet to keep healthy. This means eating foods containing a selection of proteins, carbohydrates, fibers, fats, vitamins, and minerals. Too many fatty foods or too much sugar (a type of carbohydrate) can make you unhealthy.

This cake spread with butter tastes very good, but it is full of fats and sugars.

Hamburgers are tasty treats but they are not very nourishing. Therefore, we should not eat them too often.

Salad is good for you because it is low in fat and high in vitamins.

Spaghetti contains carbohydrates for energy and protein for the growth and repair of tissue.

What does your brain do?

Without a brain, you would not be able to move, think, learn or remember, or feel anything. Your brain is the control center of your body. Information about the outside world travels along a huge network of wirelike nerves to your brain.

Nerves run all through your body. They also carry instructions from your brain to your body. The main pathway between your nerves and brain is your spinal cord. This is a long bundle of nerves running through your backbone, or spine.

When the information reaches your brain, your brain processes it and decides what action, if any, to take. It then tells your body. Your brain looks a bit like a pinkish gray lump of pudding. It is made of up to 10 billion nerve cells. It is divided up into different parts, each with a different job to do.

Parts of the brain

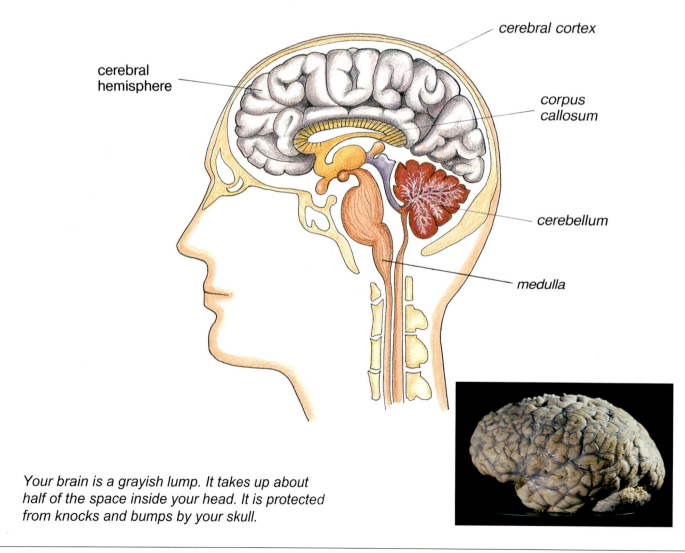

cerebral cortex

cerebral hemisphere

corpus callosum

cerebellum

medulla

Your brain is a grayish lump. It takes up about half of the space inside your head. It is protected from knocks and bumps by your skull.

Why are people left- or right-handed?

Which hand do you write with? Your left or your right? Most people write with their right hands. Only about one person in ten is left-handed.

The biggest part of your brain is called the cerebral cortex. It is divided into two halves, called hemispheres. Each hemisphere controls the opposite side of the body. The hand you write with depends on which side of your brain controls language and speech.

If the right-hand side is in control, you will be left-handed. If the left-hand side is in control, you will be right-handed. A very small number of people are ambidextrous. This means that they can write with either hand.

 Did you know?

An adult's brain weighs about three pounds. People used to think that the more intelligent a person was, the bigger his or her brain. We now know that this is not true. All adults have brains about the same size.

 See for yourself

Your brain stores some of the information it receives as memories. These may last for just a few minutes or for many years. Can you remember your first day at school, or your last birthday, or what you ate for dinner last Wednesday? Try this test to see how good your memory is.

Lay out eight objects on a table or a tray. Look at them for about 20 seconds. Now look away and see how many objects you can remember. How well have you done? Is it easier if you remember the first letters of each object, and then put the letters together as a made-up word? The letters here could make up the word *SCUMPAWS*.

SCUMPAWS

Why do you get tired?

Feeling tired is your brain and body's way of telling you that they need a rest. Your body cannot go on working hard all the time. You get used to sleeping at a regular time every night. As this time gets closer, you feel tired. You may also feel tired if you have not had enough sleep the night before or if you have been working or playing very hard. It is important to get enough sleep – it gives your body time to repair itself and to grow, and your brain time to finish processing information.

Why do you yawn?

You yawn when you are tired, when you first wake up in the morning . . . and sometimes when you are bored. Yawning is your body's way of getting a large breath of fresh air into your lungs and getting rid of a buildup of waste carbon dioxide gas. It helps stretch your chest muscles so that you can breathe more deeply.

Yawning is a **reflex action** – it is very difficult to stop. It also seems to be contagious. If you see someone else yawning, does it make you yawn, too?

 Did you know?

You probably have about five to six dreams every night. But you can usually only remember the last dream before you wake up. Sometimes you cannot remember any of your dreams at all.

 Did you know?

An adult needs about 7 to 8 hours' sleep a night. An eight-year-old child needs about 10 hours. A baby needs up to 20 hours of sleep a day.

What happens when you go to sleep?

When you go to sleep, your body slows down, although it never completely stops working. Your breathing and heartbeat slow down because your body needs less oxygen and energy when you are asleep. Your muscles relax, your digestive system slows down, and your kidneys make less urine so that you do not need to keep getting up to go to the bathroom.

Even when you sleep, your body does not stop moving. You probably shift your position in bed about 30 times a night. Your brain also changes its rate of activity. It keeps changing from deep sleep to shallow sleep. Each **cycle** of deep and shallow sleep lasts about 1.5 hours and is repeated several times a night.

If you cannot go to sleep, there are various tricks to help you relax. Try counting sheep, for a start. 1, 2, 3, 4, 5. . . .

Fast asleep at last, but your brain is still alert for signs of danger or noise in the night. If necessary, you can wake up quickly.

 ## See for yourself

If you wake up in the middle of the night, your eyes soon adjust to seeing in the dark. Your pupils, the black spots in the middles of your eyes, get bigger and wider to let as much light into your eye as possible. In bright light, however, your pupils get smaller to keep your eyes from being dazzled.

To see this in action, look into a mirror in ordinary light. Cover your eyes for a minute. Then look into the mirror again. Your pupils have become larger. They will narrow again as your eyes get used to the light. How quickly do they change size?

Dim light, pupil widens

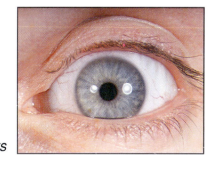

Bright light, pupil narrows

How do you see?

Sight is your most important sense. It gives you more information about the outside world than all the other senses – hearing, smell, taste, and touch – put together. You see with your eyes, two jelly-filled balls protected in socket holes in your skull.

Light passes through the front of your eye and an **image** is **projected** on to the back of the eye. You see a clear, sharp picture because the light is **focused** by a **lens**. This lens can change shape to focus light rays from distant objects or objects that are closer to it.

At the back of your eye is a layer of nerve cells called the retina. You have two types of nerve cells, called rods and cones. Rods only see in black and white. They can see quite well in dim light. Cones see in color. But they only see in good light. The light hits the rods and cones, and nerve signals are sent from your eye to your brain. They travel along a large nerve called the optic nerve. Your brain sorts out the signals and puts together the picture that you see.

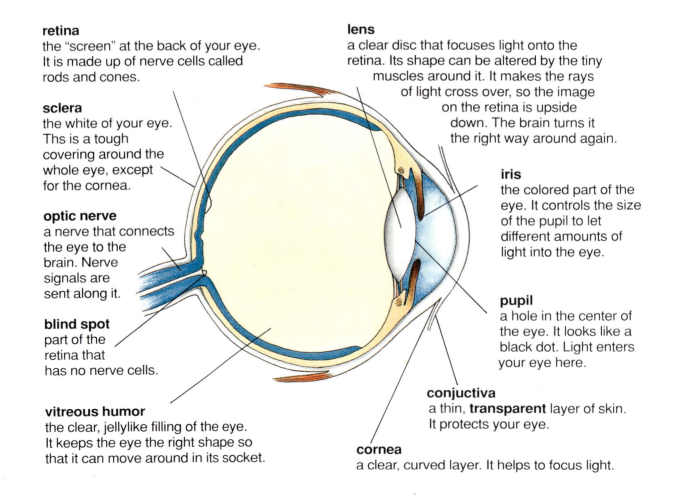

retina
the "screen" at the back of your eye. It is made up of nerve cells called rods and cones.

sclera
the white of your eye. Ths is a tough covering around the whole eye, except for the cornea.

optic nerve
a nerve that connects the eye to the brain. Nerve signals are sent along it.

blind spot
part of the retina that has no nerve cells.

vitreous humor
the clear, jellylike filling of the eye. It keeps the eye the right shape so that it can move around in its socket.

lens
a clear disc that focuses light onto the retina. Its shape can be altered by the tiny muscles around it. It makes the rays of light cross over, so the image on the retina is upside down. The brain turns it the right way around again.

iris
the colored part of the eye. It controls the size of the pupil to let different amounts of light into the eye.

pupil
a hole in the center of the eye. It looks like a black dot. Light enters your eye here.

conjuctiva
a thin, **transparent** layer of skin. It protects your eye.

cornea
a clear, curved layer. It helps to focus light.

Why do people have to wear glasses?

Do you wear glasses? Do you know anyone who wears contact lenses? People have to wear glasses or contact lenses because their eyeballs are a slightly different shape from normal and cannot focus light rays properly. Near-sighted people have longer eyeballs than normal. They can only see things at a short distance. They cannot see distant objects clearly. Far-sighted people can only see things at a long distance. They have difficulty seeing things close to them. Their eyeballs are shorter than normal. Wearing extra, artificial lenses such as glasses in front of the eyes helps the eyes to focus properly. The sight, or vision, is therefore improved.

 See for yourself

You use one of your eyes more than the other. This is called your dominant eye. Find out which is your dominant eye by holding a pencil at arm's length and lining it up with an object in the distance. Close each eye in turn, and then open them again. When one of your eyes closes, the pencil seems to jump to the side. Which eye are you closing when this happens? This is your dominant eye.

Why are people's eyes different colors?

What color are your eyes? Are they brown, blue, green, or gray? Does everyone in your family have eyes the same color? What about your friends? Which eye color is most common?

The color of your eyes depends on the amount of the **pigment**, melanin, that there is in them. Melanin is also the substance that colors your skin and hair. (See page 42.) Brown eyes contain a lot of melanin. Blue eyes have very little. But the amount of melanin, and therefore the color of your eyes, is inherited, or passed down, from your parents.

For each of your features, such as the color of your eyes or hair, your height and build, you have 2 genes. One comes from your mother, the other from your father. Genes are special sets of instructions found in your cells. You look the way you do because of these genes. Some genes are stronger than others. If you inherit one brown-eye gene and one blue-eye gene, you will probably have brown eyes because the brown gene is stronger. If you inherit 2 blue genes, you will have blue eyes. Sometimes there are exceptions to this.

What does color-blind mean?

Some people cannot see certain colors properly. They are known as "color-blind." This is caused by the cones in the eye not working normally. (See page 32.) Most color-blind people cannot see red and green properly because the cones detecting red and green are faulty. Like eye color, color-blindness is inherited from your parents. Men are more likely to be color-blind than women. About 1 in 12 men but only 1 in 200 women are color-blind.

 Did you know?

Some people cannot see colors at all. Their cones do not work, so they can only see in black and white. Fortunately, this is rare. It only affects about 1 in 40,000 people.

See for yourself

When you visit the optician's for an eye test, you might also be given a color-blindness test. You can do this test for yourself by looking at the dots in these circles. Which numbers can you see?

If you can see the number 96, you have normal color vision. If you cannot see a number at all, you may be red-green color-blind.

If you can see the number 5, your color vision is normal. If you cannot see a number at all, you may have a defect in your vision.

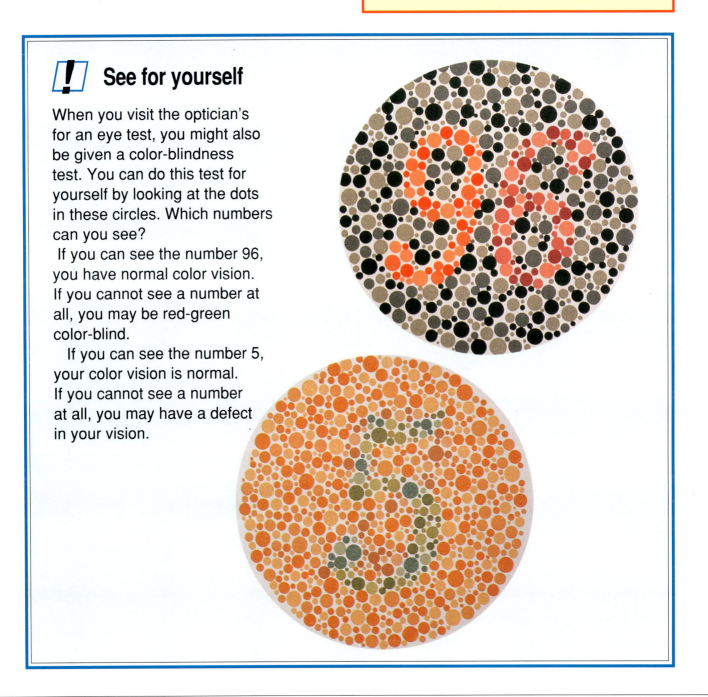

What makes you cry?

Lots of things make you cry. You might cry if you are very sad or very happy, if you have hurt yourself, or if you have been chopping onions. No one really knows why these things make you cry. But we do know how you cry.

Your eyes make soothing liquid to keep them from drying out and to clean away dust or germs. Tears are made all the time in special **glands** in your eyes. The tears normally wash over your eyes and then drain away through tiny holes, called tear ducts, in the corners of your eyes.

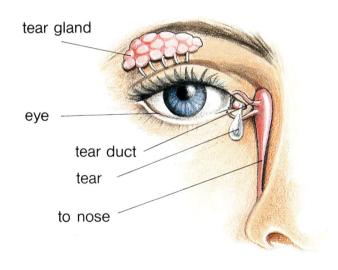

tear gland

eye

tear duct

tear

to nose

If you get a speck of dust in your eye, you make more tears than normal to get rid of the irritation. Your tear ducts cannot cope with the extra fluid and so they overflow, making you cry. The same thing happens if you are sad, upset, happy, or hurt.

Why are tears salty?

Your eyes are very delicate and can easily become infected. Tears help to wash away germs and keep your eyes clean and healthy. Being salty makes the tears more efficient at killing germs and cleaning the eyes.

What does blinking do?

When you blink, your eyelids move across your eye and spread the tear fluid over its surface. You also blink if something brushes against your eyelashes. Your eyelid shuts down over your eye, preventing dust, germs, or other unwelcome intruders from getting in. Blinking is an automatic, reflex action – you cannot stop yourself from doing it.

How do you hear sounds?

Sounds are made up of vibrations in the air, called sound waves. Low sounds are caused by slow vibrations and high sounds by fast vibrations. Your outer ear makes sure that the vibrations go into your ear, where they travel down the ear canal to the eardrum. This is a thin sheet of skinlike membrane across the end of the canal. The membrane is stretched tight, a bit like a drum skin. When the sound waves hit it, it vibrates, too. These vibrations are passed on to three tiny bones deep inside your ear. They are called the anvil, hammer, and stirrup because of their shapes.

From here, vibrations travel to your cochlea. This is a coiled, snaillike tube filled with liquid. Special cells turn the vibrations into electrical signals that are sent to your brain along the auditory nerve. This nerve connects the ear to the brain. Your brain sorts the signals into the sounds you hear.

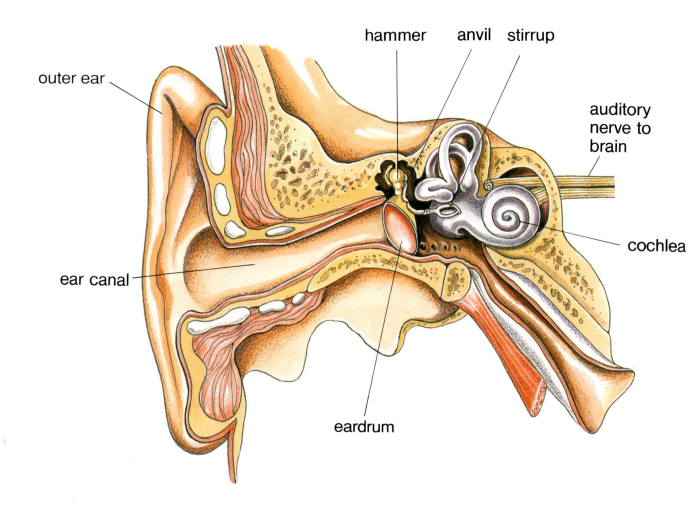

People can hear a wide range of sounds, from a quiet whisper to the roar of a jet plane. Children usually have more sensitive ears than adults.

Why do you feel dizzy?

Your ears also contain special parts that help you to balance. These are tubes called the semicircular canals, which are filled with fluid. There are three of these tubes in each ear. They are lined with nerve cells. When you move your head, the fluid inside the canals moves and touches the nerve ends. They send signals to your brain to tell it about the change in your head's position.

If you spin around and around, then stop, the fluid in the canals keeps moving. This sends confused messages to your brain. When you stop spinning, your muscles and eyes tell your brain that your body has stopped. The fluid tells it that your body is still spinning. This is why you feel dizzy for a while.

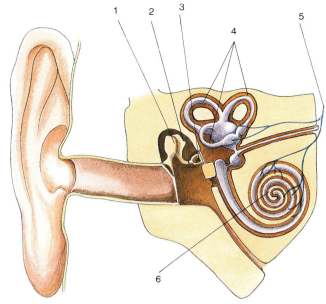

1. hammer
2. anvil
3. stirrup
4. semicircular canals
5. auditory nerve to brain
6. cochlea

The liquid inside your semicircular canals is called endolymph.

 See for yourself

You can test your balance for yourself. Choose an object, such as a clock hanging on the wall. Close your eyes, then point at it. Keep pointing and open your eyes. Were you still pointing at the clock? How near were you?

Now spin around twice, then close your eyes and try to point at the clock again. You are probably way off this time because your sense of balance has been confused by the spinning.

You must now be wondering how skaters and ballet dancers can spin around so many times and so fast. Skaters and ballet dancers focus on fixed points as they spin, to keep themselves from feeling dizzy. This is called spotting.

How do you smell things?

Smells are made of tiny, invisible chemicals floating in the air. As you breathe in, the smells travel up your nostrils. They are then picked up by a small patch of smell **sensors** in your nasal cavity, the hollow space inside your nose. The sensors have special cells, covered in slimy mucus, that absorb the smells from the air. Then they send signals along your olfactory nerve, which connects the smell sensors to your brain. Your brain processes the signals and tells you what sort of smell it is and if it is pleasant or nasty.

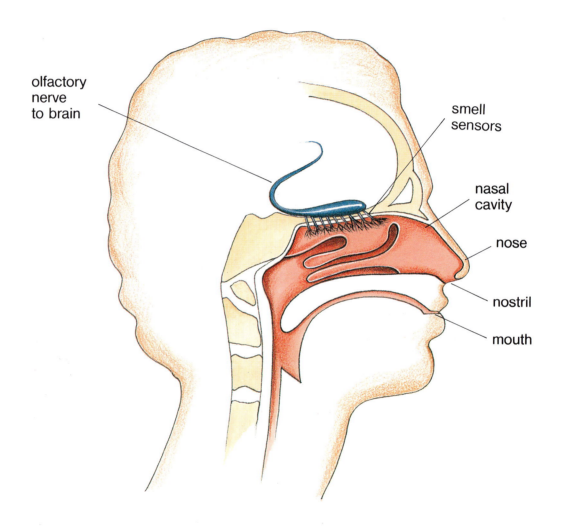

olfactory nerve to brain

smell sensors

nasal cavity

nose

nostril

mouth

Your smell sensors in your nasal cavity only cover an area about the size of a postage stamp.

 Did you know?

Your sense of smell is about 10,000 times stronger than your sense of taste.

Why do people sniff at things?

Sniffing helps you to smell things better. In normal breathing, only a little air, and therefore only a few smell particles, floats up into your nasal cavity to be picked up by your smell sensors. A long, hard sniff pulls more air and more smell particles toward your smell sensors to give you a stronger smell.

 Did you know?

Human beings can tell the difference between about 3,000 smells. But this is nothing compared with the sensitivity of a dog's nose. A German shepherd can smell about 1 million times better than we can.

The top left-hand picture shows a test tube full of decaying food that is being used in an experiment. It has a terrible smell. Your sense of smell tells you if your food is good or bad. The bad smell of the food in the test tube warns you that it should not be eaten. The pleasant smell of the meal below makes you want to eat it.

How do you taste things?

What is your favorite taste? Is it something sweet or something sour? When you eat something, your tongue tastes it. It tells you if your food is hot or cold, if it tastes good or bad, and about its flavor.

Different flavors are detected by tiny taste buds on your tongue. You have more than 10,000 taste buds in your mouth. They look like tiny bulges. Most are on your tongue. But there are also some on the inside of your cheeks, on the roof of your mouth, and in your throat.

Taste buds can taste four different flavors – sweet, sour, salty, and bitter. On different parts of your tongue, they can pick up different flavors.

Taste buds pick up flavors that mix with the saliva, or spit, that you make as you eat. Then nerves carry messages about the tastes to your brain.

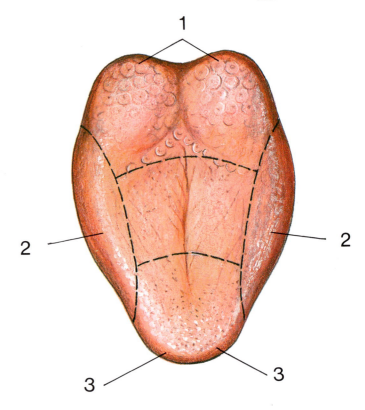

1. *bitter flavors*
2. *sour flavors*
3. *sweet and salty flavors*

Your tongue is a large piece of muscle. It helps you taste your food and break it up into pieces small enough for you to swallow.

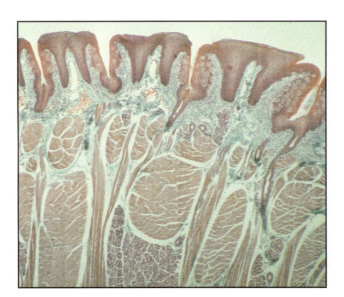

Your taste buds look like tiny bulges on the surface of your tongue.

! See for yourself

Your senses of taste and smell often work together. If you have a cold and cannot smell, you probably will not be able to taste your food very well, either. Try this test.

Blindfold a friend. Then hold a piece of onion under his or her nose. Give your friend various pieces of food to eat, such as bread, potato, or a slice of apple. Can your friend tell what he or she is eating? Or does the onion smell confuse the person?

How do you feel things?

You touch or feel things with your skin. Your skin touches the things around you. It can feel if something light or heavy is pressing on it. It can feel different textures, such as rough or smooth, and heat and cold and pain.

Your skin is made up of 2 layers – the epidermis and the dermis. The epidermis is the top layer of hard, dead cells. Below it lies the dermis. This layer contains millions of tiny nerve sensors. Each type is sensitive to a different type of touch and sends signals about it to your brain. Your brain **interprets** the signals and you feel the result. Sensors all over your body send millions of signals every second to your brain.

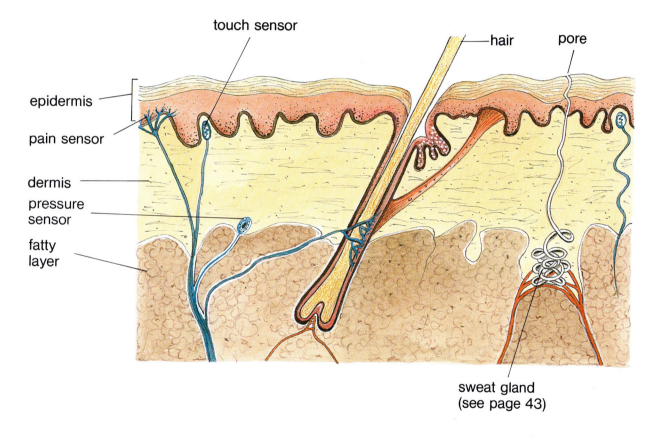

touch sensor — hair — pore

epidermis

pain sensor

dermis

pressure sensor

fatty layer

sweat gland (see page 43)

! See for yourself

Your skin is more sensitive in some places than others. This is because there are more sensors in some places than others. Test this by taping 2 pencils to a ruler, about $1/2$ inch apart. Ask a friend to close his or her eyes. Then touch him or her gently with the pencils on the fingertips, arm, neck, and so on. How many points can the person feel each time? In sensitive places, the person should feel the 2 points. In less sensitive places, the person will feel just 1 point. The most sensitive skin should be on the fingertips, toes, and lips.

Why do people have different-colored skin?

The color of your skin depends on how much of the brown pigment, melanin, it contains. Melanin also gives your eyes and hair their color. (See pages 33 and 45.) Dark skin contains a lot of melanin. Pale skin contains very little. Melanin is made by cells at the base of your epidermis. People with the condition of albinism cannot make melanin. They have white hair, pale eyes, and very pale skin.

Melanin helps protect your skin from the sun's harmful ultraviolet (UV) rays. This is why people who come from hot countries usually have dark skin. It is also why you may get a tan if you stay in the sun for a few hours, because the cells at the base of the epidermis make more of the protective melanin.

 Did you know?

An adult's skin covers an area of about 21.5 square feet and weighs 6 to 7 pounds. Your skin is about $1/16$ inch thick on most of your body. On your eyelids, however, it is just $1/64$ inch thick, and on the soles of your feet it is $1/4$ inch thick.

These children all have different amounts of melanin in their skin.

Why do your fingers get wrinkled in the bath?

Your skin is covered in a natural oil called sebum. It keeps your skin smooth and waterproof. It also helps stop fluids from going out of your skin and drying it up. If you keep your hands in water, the oil washes off and your skin becomes wrinkled. Dry your hands, rub in a little hand cream, and your skin will become smooth again.

What makes you sweat?

Hot weather or hard exercise can make you sweat. This is one of your body's automatic ways of trying to cool you down. Salty, watery sweat is made in curly tubes, called sweat glands, deep under your skin. You can see one of these glands on page 41. The sweat seeps up the tubes and out of tiny

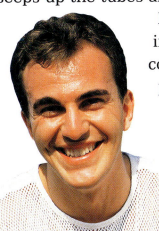

holes, called pores, in your skin. Sweat cools your body by a process called evaporation. This means that the liquid water in sweat turns into invisible water vapor. As it evaporates, it draws heat away from your body and cools you down.

 Did you know?

You have up to five million sweat glands in your body. On a hot day, you may make over 2 quarts of sweat. Even on a cool day, you make almost $1/2$ pint of sweat.

Why do you look flushed?

Flushing has the opposite effect of goose pimples. (See page 45.) It is designed to cool you down. When you get too hot, the tiny blood vessels in your skin get wider. More blood is able to flow through them close to the surface of the skin. This means it can be cooled by the air outside you, which draws the heat away from you. If you have pale skin, you look red because of the extra blood. The same thing sometimes happens when you get angry or embarrassed. Then it is called blushing.

 See for yourself

You can see how evaporation works by dipping one of your hands in warm water. Shake off any excess water. Leave the other hand dry. Get a friend or an adult to blow on each of your hands with a hair dryer. Which one feels cooler? It should be the wet hand, as the water evaporates and draws heat away with it.

Why do you have hair?

Our prehistoric ancestors were much hairier than we are. Their hair helped keep them warm. The hair trapped heat next to their skin and stopped the warmth from being lost from their bodies into the air. This is exactly how an animal's fur works.

You still have hair all over your body, but most of it is very fine and almost invisible. You do not need such thick hair because you have clothes and heating in your home to keep you warm. But the patches of hair that you still have do an important job.

The hair on your head helps protect your scalp from sunburn and stops heat from escaping. Your eyebrows stop sweat from dripping down into your eyes and your eyelashes help protect your eyes from dust and dirt.

Hair is made from a protein called keratin. Our nails and skin, as well as animals' horns, scales, and claws, are also made from keratin. The keratin cells in hair are dead, which is why it does not hurt when you have your hair cut.

 Did you know?

You have about 100,000 hairs on your head and about 5 million on your whole body.

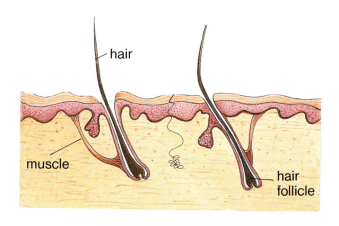

Hair comes in many shades, textures, and styles.

What makes hair curly or straight?

What is your hair like? Is it wavy, straight, or curly? The shape of the hair follicles causes the different types of hair. A follicle is the tiny pit from which the root of the hair grows. If your hair is wavy, it means that your follicles are flat and oblong shaped. If your hair is straight, then your follicles are round. If it is curly, then your follicles are oval.

Why are some people bald?

As they get older, some people become bald. Their hair falls out and new hairs are not made to replace them. Baldness may also be inherited, or passed down from parent to child. If a father is bald, it is likely that his sons will become bald when they get older.

⚠ See for yourself

Hairs usually live for about two to three years. Then they fall out and the follicles have a few months' rest before producing a new hair. People lose about 70 hairs from their heads every day. See how many hairs you lose over a week. Brush your hair in the morning and evening and count the number of hairs that fall out.

Why do people go gray?

Older people tend to have gray or white hair. This is because they produce less melanin, the pigment that gives hair its color. White hair contains no melanin at all. Going gray is also inherited. If a mother or father goes gray when they are young, it is quite likely that their sons and daughters will do so as well.

Why do you get goose pimples?

Goose pimples are one of your body's ways of trying to warm you up when you get cold. When a furry animal gets cold, its hair stands on end. The hair traps air next to the animal's body and keeps it warm, like an extra blanket.

When you get cold, your hair tries to do the same thing. It does not really help warm you up because you do not have enough hair. But the tiny muscles that pull the hairs up also pull up little bunches of skin. These are called goose pimples.

Goose pimples appear automatically when you get cold. Shivering is another automatic reaction to try to get you warm. It is more useful because your muscles do make some extra heat in the form of energy as they twitch.

Glossary

absorbed   soaked in, like a sponge soaking in water

alveoli (alveolus)   air sacs in the lungs

automatic reaction   something that is done instantly, without thinking

blood vessels   tiny threadlike tubes that carry blood around the body

body tissue   groups of the same type of cell

cycle   when things happen in the same way and always go around to the same beginning each time, like a circle

digested   when food has been broken down into small enough pieces to be absorbed into the bloodstream

enzymes   chemicals made by living cells that can break down food into nutrients

filter   something that separates the things that you want from those things that you do not want, rather like a sieve

focused   when the edges of shapes are clearly seen and do not look blurred

glands   groups of cells that make special fluids, occurring in many different parts of your body

glucose   a simple carbohydrate, or energy giver

image   picture

interprets   explains

lens   a clear material through which light can pass and that can bend the rays of light

nutrients   the goodness from food that keeps you healthy and helps you to grow: the vitamins, minerals, and energy givers

pigment   coloring

projected   thrown onto

protein   the body's building or repair material

reflex action   an automatic response to something, such as when your hand moves away quickly when it touches something hot

sensor   something that can detect, or feel, different conditions, such as rough or smooth, hot or cold, soft or hard, etc.

starch   energy-giving compounds found in rice, potatoes, spaghetti, bread, and so on

supple   something that is soft and can change its shape

transparent   completely clear

urine   a liquid that carries waste products from your kidneys and out of your body

vibrate   to make very quick, quivering movements

waste products   things that cannot be used

Further reading

Avraham, Regina. **The Circulatory System.** New York: Chelsea House, 1989.

Berger, Gilda. **The Human Body.** New York: Doubleday, 1989.

Parker, Steve. **Skeleton.** (Eyewitness Books). New York: Alfred A. Knopf, 1988.

Parker, Steve and Brian Ward. **The Human Body** series. (revised edition)
   New York: Franklin Watts.

Simon & Schuster Pocket Book of the Human Body. New York:
   Little Simon Books, 1987.

Index

(Humans)